The Alden Family Mysteries
by Gertrude Chandler Warner

THE BOXCAR CHILDREN
SURPRISE ISLAND
THE YELLOW HOUSE MYSTERY
MYSTERY RANCH
MIKE'S MYSTERY
BLUE BAY MYSTERY
THE WOODSHED MYSTERY
THE LIGHTHOUSE MYSTERY
MOUNTAIN TOP MYSTERY
SCHOOLHOUSE MYSTERY
CABOOSE MYSTERY
HOUSEBOAT MYSTERY
SNOWBOUND MYSTERY
TREE HOUSE MYSTERY
BICYCLE MYSTERY
MYSTERY IN THE SAND
MYSTERY BEHIND THE WALL
BUS STATION MYSTERY
BENNY UNCOVERS A MYSTERY

Schoolhouse Mystery

Gertrude Chandler Warner

Illustrations: David Cunningham

ALBERT WHITMAN & COMPANY, NILES, ILLINOIS

ISBN 0-8075-7263-2

 Published simultaneously in Canada by General Publishing, Limited, Toronto.

7 9 10 8 6

Printed in the U.S.A.

Contents

CHAPTER 1

Benny's Plan

The whole Alden family sat on the front porch reading. It was one of those hot vacation days in June. Supper was over and the sun had not yet set.

"Plenty of light to read by," said Benny as he took his favorite book to his favorite seat in the corner. Jessie and Violet, his sisters, were already sitting in the porch swing. Henry, the oldest of the Aldens, was just home from college. He sat in one easy chair, and Grandfather sat in another.

Suddenly Grandfather looked up. Benny was not reading any more. He was looking straight ahead. But he was not looking at anything.

"What's the matter, Ben?" asked Mr. Alden.

"I'm thinking," said Benny. He did not move.

"What are you thinking about, old man?" asked Henry. "It seems to be important."

"No, it isn't important," Benny said, but he did not go back to his book.

"You might as well tell us," said his older sister Jessie. "It must be interesting."

Violet added, "Please, Benny."

"Well," said Benny, "it's something Max said."

"Oh, your friend Max?" said Henry. "What did Max say?"

"Well, it wasn't much," said Benny, "but it got me thinking. He said that we Aldens always seem to have an exciting time on vacation no matter where we go. Always some adventure."

"Max was right," said Violet.

"Yes," said Benny, looking at Violet. "I told Max he was dead right. But then he said he'd like to see us have any exciting adventures if we went to his father's favorite fishing town up on the northern coast. He said it was a tiny village with nothing there. He is sure we couldn't go there and have any adventures. He said even an Alden couldn't find anything exciting in that place."

Mr. Alden was quick to read Benny's mind. He laughed and said, "So I suppose you want to go to this fishing village and try it?"

Benny turned and looked at his grandfather. "Well," he said, "you see it sounded pretty interesting. I mean I can't imagine being dull anywhere, can you?"

"No, Benny, I can't," said Mr. Alden. "This is not a family to have a dull time. It never was. How would you like to go there for a short time? There would still be half the summer left to go somewhere else."

"Oh, I remember!" said Jessie. "You had something all planned for this summer, Grandfather."

"It can wait," Mr. Alden said, smiling to himself.

"It certainly would be fun to visit a dull town," said Jessie. "Is it right on the sea?"

"Yes," said Benny. "It's an island at high tide with water on all sides. But at low tide the ocean goes out and leaves a roadway made of rocks and gravel. You can drive a car across or walk across. But the people don't go off the island very often, Max says. Just the summer visitors."

"And I guess there are not many of them," said Henry.

"Where do the visitors stay?" asked Violet.

"There's only one place," Benny answered. "It's something like an old country hotel with six rooms for summer fishermen like Max's father. The village is tiny. There's a schoolhouse and a store. There isn't even a post office. There are houses for the people who live there, and a sardine factory where they work. They use the schoolhouse for town meetings. And that's all."

Grandfather looked around at the family. "If you all want to go, I'm ready. But every one of you must want to go."

"Of course we do, Grandfather," said Henry. "It will be fun to prove old Max is wrong. We have exciting times just by ourselves."

"We'll show Max!" said Benny.

Henry added, "It would be interesting to study a

village where people are so cut off from everyone else. I might even write a college paper on it."

"What's the name of this village?" asked Grandfather. "Maybe I know it from my old fishing trips."

"Maybe you do," said Benny. "You know a lot of things. It is called Port Elizabeth."

Mr. Alden shook his head. "No, I don't know that name. We can look for it on a map. It can't be too far away."

Violet ran into the house and soon came back with a book of maps. "You look it up," said Grandfather.

"Here it is," cried Violet. "It must be very small, the name is in such fine print. And here's the island. The only town near it is Northport."

Henry looked at the map. "It looks as if Northport is about thirty miles away," he said. "It must be a very small town, too."

"It's bigger than Port Elizabeth, though," Jessie said. "We can probably buy things there."

"We can take some things with us, too," said Grandfather.

Benny began to laugh. "I never thought you would

want to go to Max's village," he said. "I just can't help thinking about the surprise we'll have for Max."

"Neither can I," said Henry. "We'll let Benny tell Max when we get home what a dull time we had."

"You seem to be very sure you will have an adventure," said Grandfather, his eyes twinkling. "What happens if it is dull, just as Max said?"

"Let's try it anyway, Grandfather," said Jessie. "If it is dull, we won't mind."

Violet said, "I'll take my watercolors. I love to paint the sea."

Henry winked at Benny and said, "We'll find something to do. We can always fish."

Just a week later Henry drove the station wagon into the fishing village of Port Elizabeth. The tide was out. It was exactly as Max had said. There was the old hotel with six rooms, the schoolhouse, and a small store. They knew that the storekeeper, Mr. Fenton, owned the hotel. He had rented them three rooms by telephone.

"Shall we go to the store first?" asked Henry.

"Yes, I'm sure Mr. Fenton will have the keys. We

can let him know we have arrived," said Grandfather. "I hope the beds are comfortable."

Everyone was surprised when Mr. Fenton opened the door of the first room. They had not expected anything so pleasant. There were two comfortable beds. The floor was bare except for two handmade rugs near the beds.

"Very good, very good," said Mr. Alden nodding his head at the storekeeper. "I can see that we are going to enjoy this."

"It's lovely," said Violet. "It's just right for us."

"Now," said Mr. Fenton, "I'm going to show you something I don't show all my guests. It's a kitchen."

He opened another door at the end of the hall, and, sure enough, there was a small kitchen. There was a large table in the middle of the room. The sink and stove were old fashioned, but the refrigerator looked new. There were cupboards full of dishes.

"It will be a pleasure to let you use it," Mr. Fenton said. "There's no place to eat in Port Elizabeth, and you'd have to go to Northport for your meals—and that's thirty miles away."

"Oh, aren't you kind!" cried Jessie, "A kitchen like this is just what we need."

"Can you cook?" asked Mr. Fenton.

"They all can cook, even Benny," said Mr. Alden, laughing. "I tell them they can make something out of nothing."

"Good," said Mr. Fenton. "I thought you people looked as if you could take care of yourselves. I'm pretty good at guessing what people are like. Don't often make a mistake. That's why I showed you the kitchen."

"Today we brought our own supper," said Benny. "We didn't know about the kitchen."

"That's fine," said Mr. Fenton. "You must be tired. You have had a long drive. Maybe you'll go to bed early and start up again tomorrow."

"We'll just drive around and see the town first," said Mr. Alden.

"It won't take you long," said Mr. Fenton with a laugh. "It's a very small place."

Henry drove slowly along the sandy road by the ocean. Two large wharves stood out in the water.

The sardine factory could be seen in the distance, but it was closed for the day. Some boats were tied up there. Beyond the factory was a high cliff, and on top was a very large and beautiful old house.

"I wonder who lives in that house," said Benny. "Isn't it huge? Must be a big family. I guess there are twenty rooms."

"It looks to me like an old family mansion," said Grandfather. "It is certainly not new. The house seems to be closed, too."

It was not, but the Aldens did not know that until later. The road curved around past the cliff, past the store and a row of fishermen's houses, and back to the hotel. That was all there was to see, except for the schoolhouse. A great many bushes and trees stood between the schoolhouse and their hotel.

The schoolhouse had once been painted white, but much of the paint had worn off. On top there was a belfry with a bell in it.

"Listen!" said Benny. "Is that the school bell ringing?"

"Oh, Benny!" Jessie said. "What an imagination!"

Violet looked hard at the building. She said, "I think it's a pretty little school. That big chimney is a queer shape, isn't it?"

And so it proved to be.

"We have done the town," said Grandfather. "That is all there is. Maybe Max is right, Benny, and it is dull."

"Well, maybe," said Benny. "We haven't been here very long. Anyway I'm hungry."

"You shouldn't be hungry," said Jessie. She looked at her watch. Then she looked up in surprise. "It's half past five!" she exclaimed. "I thought it was about three o'clock."

"It's a long time since we stopped for lunch," said Henry. "Let's get unpacked and have supper."

The girls were delighted. They put the straw basket on the kitchen table and opened it. They took out chicken sandwiches, pickles, cheese, doughnuts, and potato chips. Benny ran over to the store to get cold milk.

Grandfather had hardly had time to unpack when he heard Violet call, "Supper!"

The children sat on long benches, but Grandfather had a chair at the head of the table.

"This reminds me of Surprise Island," said Henry. "Only there we didn't have a real table. We used two barrels with a board across them."

"One thing is the same," said Benny. "I'm starved. Let's begin!"

Everyone else must have been hungry, too. The food was soon gone. Then the boys went to their room to unpack, and the girls to another. Grandfather had a big room alone.

The hotel was so near the ocean that the splash of the waves kept them awake for a while. But they loved the sound of waves and quickly fell asleep.

The Aldens did not know that soon they would meet a wonderful friend and find some people who were not friendly at all.

CHAPTER 2

Being Watched

The next day the Aldens began in earnest to learn more about Port Elizabeth.

First they walked over to the little store. They found that they could buy almost any kind of food there. The girls bought enough food to last for a few days. Then Benny asked Mr. Fenton, "Who lives in the big mansion on the cliff?"

"Well," said Mr. Fenton, "Miss Gray lives there. Miss Elizabeth Gray. She is the last of her family."

"She lives alone in that great house?" cried Benny.

"No, not really alone. She has a woman to get her meals and a man to mow the grass and shovel snow in the winter. But she has no family. Her grandfather built that house, and twelve children grew up there. But some of them died and some left. She hasn't anyone close to her. People say she writes books."

Jessie said, "I should think she would be very lonesome. Does she ever go out?"

"No," said Mr. Fenton. He shook his head. "Almost never. Nobody calls there, either. She is shy, and people don't feel comfortable with her. She has plenty of money, and she has done a lot for the town. Her grandfather built the schoolhouse many years ago. He called it the Elizabeth Gray School for his wife, Miss Gray's grandmother. Miss Gray is the one who has the schoolhouse cleaned in the fall, and she keeps the keys. But she stays by herself."

"I'm sorry for anyone like that," said Benny. "She must miss a lot of fun."

As the Alden family talked with the storekeeper, a red-haired boy and girl came in together. They looked alike and were certainly twins.

The island children did not look at the Aldens. In fact, they looked the other way. But Benny thought,

"They must have looked us over before they came in."

"We want some flour," said the boy. "And Ma wants some more tea." His voice was as rough as his looks. His sister looked rough, too. Her hair hung in wisps around her face.

The girl counted out the money carefully, but she did it slowly. It seemed hard for her, so at last Mr. Fenton helped her. When they had gone, Mr. Fenton said, "To tell you the truth, Mr. Alden, I'm sorry for the children who are brought up here. Living is hard on this island, and the people have no education. The children never have a chance to learn any other way to live. They don't even have TV. They don't see magazines, and they never go off this island."

"Oh, dear," said Jessie, "I shouldn't think they would know anything about the world."

"They don't," said Mr. Fenton. "As soon as they're old enough, they work in the sardine factory. Those two are the Moss twins. They work in the factory whenever it is open."

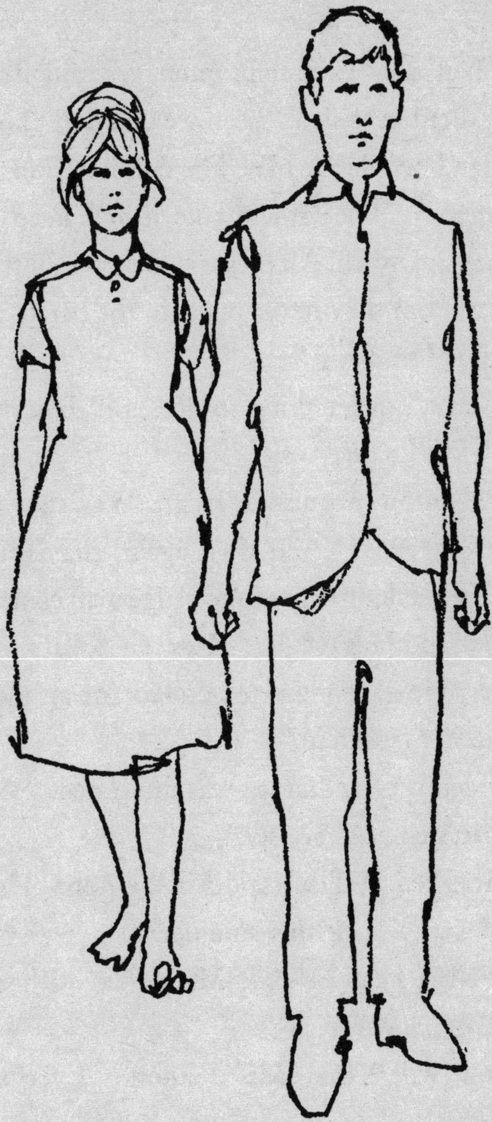

"Then they earn some money," said Benny.

Mr. Fenton smiled. "I can see you don't know what the island people are like. The children don't ever see that money. The fathers take it and keep it. They don't spend much. All these people save all the money they can, but they never put it in the bank. They put it in an old stocking."

"That's a queer thing to do," said Benny. "They might lose it that way."

Mr. Fenton gave a short laugh. "Yes, they certainly might," he said. "And then again, they might not! Here's something funny. A strange man came here last summer and he gave Mr. Moss ten dollars for an old quarter. He gave me three dollars for an old penny, but I didn't trust him."

Suddenly Grandfather was interested. "What was this man's name?" he asked.

"Mr. Fred Willet," said Mr. Fenton. "He said he would come back this summer."

"Well, if he does," said Mr. Alden, "I hope to see him."

"You will," said Mr. Fenton. "Everyone will

see Freddy Willet if he's around. He's very friendly. I'll say that much for him."

Then Jessie paid for the groceries and thanked Mr. Fenton for telling them about the island. Henry and Benny raced home to the hotel to put the food away.

Violet said, "Imagine how it would be to live on this island and not know anything else."

"I can't imagine," said Jessie. "I don't blame that girl if she can't count very well."

When the boys came back, they and the girls went down to the beach. Mr. Alden did not go this time. He had to write some letters.

As the young people walked along, Violet said, "I have a funny feeling that people are staring at us."

"Me, too," said Benny. "And how is it we don't see any men around? I see kids and some women, but not a single man. I thought a lot of fishermen lived here. But where are they?"

Henry looked all around. "You're right, Ben. I hadn't really noticed. But I think I know the answer. If the men are fishermen, they must be out in their boats."

"Let's go down to the wharf and see what is going on," said Benny.

There were people on the beach. There were many children of all ages and some mothers. Some of the older girls and boys were sitting on the sand working on nets. They tied knot after knot. They all worked fast. They did not look up when the Aldens went by.

Little children were playing in the water. They all swam like fishes. Some boys dived off the wharf into deep water.

"Aren't you afraid to be under water?" Benny asked a small boy.

"No, I like it. I can always come up," the boy said. He seemed surprised that anyone would ask him such a question.

"I can see you are a fine swimmer," Benny told him. "Probably you've been swimming all your life."

Henry laughed. He said, "Probably all these children can swim as soon as they can walk."

Jessie smiled and said hello to a woman who was knitting. The woman answered gruffly, but she quickly looked the other way.

When the Aldens went home for lunch, Jessie said to her grandfather, "These people aren't very friendly, are they?"

"No," said Mr. Alden. "They don't trust strangers. I've seen people like this before."

Benny frowned. "What have we done wrong?" he asked.

"Nothing," said Mr. Alden. "You'll just have to get used to the idea that these people have different ways."

Benny said, "Well, even if they do, I should think they could smile."

"Do you want to go home?" Grandfather asked.

"Oh, no, not yet!" said all four Aldens together. Then they laughed, for they had all agreed to keep trying.

Grandfather smiled. He liked to see his grandchildren stick to something that was not easy.

It was lucky that the Aldens could not hear what people were saying about them. The people had watched them quietly ever since they had come.

One girl said, "They're stuck-up rich kids. Look at their clothes! I bet those girls never had to work."

Some of the older people said, "Summer people! We've seen plenty of them. I wish we had half the money they spend."

"That car is air-conditioned," said a big boy. "Showing off, they are."

But his mother spoke up. "I don't think they're stuck-up. And I don't think they're showing off. They all smile and act friendly. You are just jealous."

It was true. The island children wished they were like the Aldens with nothing to do. They watched them every minute. They could hear the four young people laughing and talking together as they went around the town.

But as time passed, things began to change. People began to like the Aldens. They were such pleasant visitors. The island children really wanted to be friends, but not one of them knew how to say so.

CHAPTER 3

Wanted: A Schoolhouse

It was a few days later, and the girls were getting lunch. Grandfather came in from the store. He said, "While you were at the beach Mr. Fenton told me that the fishermen get up at three o'clock in the morning to take their boats out. That's why we never see any men in the morning."

Henry said, "Well, we know they come back at four or five in the afternoon. We've noticed that every day."

"They look fine coming in one by one," said Benny. "I'm going down to the beach to watch those boats. I don't care if nobody speaks to me. But I'm going early. I don't want to miss anything."

Long before three o'clock the four Aldens went down to the sandy beach. Violet took her watercolors, brushes, and paper.

A few boats were coming in early. The fishermen started to shovel fish into boxes. Some of the fish were spread out in nets to dry. Others were packed in ice to go to Northport. Gulls were flying all around the wharf, trying to get leftover fish. They made a great noise.

"Fish smells awful, doesn't it?" said Benny.

"Well, there is so much of it the whole town smells of fish," said Henry. "I suppose it is the fish drying that smells."

Just then the red-haired girl and her brother came slowly out of their house next to the store. They passed the Aldens.

"Oh, hello there!" said Jessie.

"Hello," said the girl, but she did not stop. In fact she seemed to walk faster.

Jessie said sadly, "Nobody wants to be friends."

"Maybe Max is right," said Benny. "It will be dull if nobody is friendly."

"Come on, Ben, don't give up so easily," Henry said. "If anyone can make friends, you can."

After Violet had watched the boats for a while, she climbed up on the rocks. She could see the harbor better from there. The other Aldens stayed on the sand below.

"Oh, my!" Violet called down. "There are a lot of small pools of seawater all over the top of this rock. I'm going to use salt water for my watercolors!" So she washed her brushes in a pool of seawater.

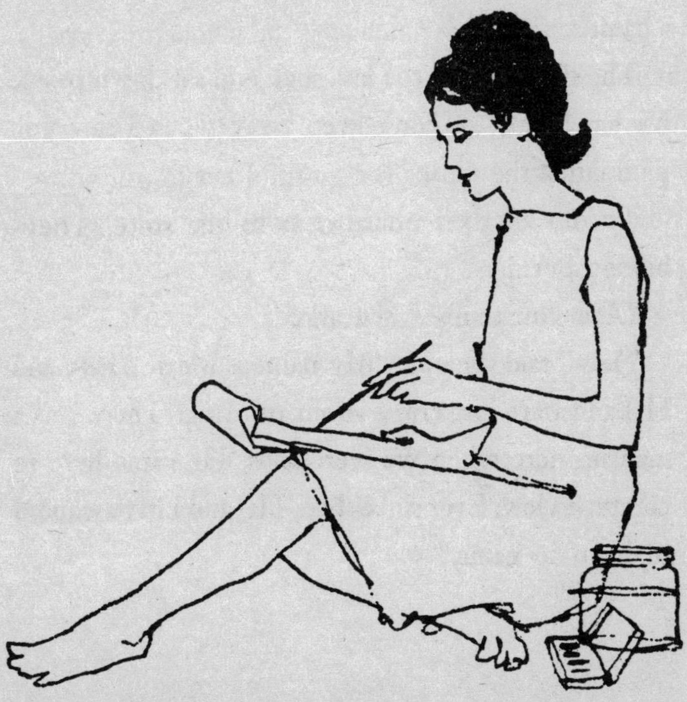

She had just painted a blue band for the sea and some yellow sand, when she heard someone climbing up the rock behind her. She knew her family was sitting on the sand below her because she could see them. Who could this be? She turned her head to look. It was the red-haired girl!

"Oh, can I watch you? Do you mind?" asked the girl.

Violet was so surprised she could hardly answer. But she said, "Of course I don't mind! I'm not much of a painter, though."

The girl climbed the last rock and sat down beside Violet. "I just couldn't keep away when I saw you painting!" she said.

Then Violet saw that her twin brother was right behind her.

"Are you twins?" she asked.

"Yes," said the girl. "My name is Marie Moss, and Hal and I are just crazy about painting! There was a man up here when we were kids. He came here to paint the view. Ever since then, Hal and I have wanted to learn to paint."

"Did the man show you how?" asked Violet. She looked from one to the other.

"Him? Oh, no! He chased us away," said Hal with a frown. "He didn't like to have us watch him."

Marie said, "He didn't stay here long. He painted just two pictures. One was of the harbor and one was our house. They were beautiful!"

"Then I guess you did watch him," said Violet.

"Yes, we did," said Hal. "The man never guessed. We knew the rocks better than he did. So we got behind a rock only a few feet away. We saw everything he did. We saw just what colors he used. He had oil paints."

"And you remember all this time!" said Violet.

"Oh, yes!" said Marie. "He mixed a lovely blue with green. It looked just exactly like the water. Then he put purple in it! See? Under the rocks, it's purple."

"You know," said Violet slowly, "you see things the way an artist would. Did you ever have any paints?"

"No," said Hal. "We tried to make pictures with old crayons. But if we only had some paints—!"

The other Aldens heard what was going on. They climbed up the rocks and sat down.

"Are you going to stay very long?" asked Marie.

"Well, I think so," said Jessie, smiling. "We like it here."

"You see," began the boy and stopped. He seemed to be having trouble with his words.

"Did you want something?" asked Benny.

The two strangers laughed a little. The girl said, "I guess we are scared."

Benny said, "Say! You can't be scared of us, can you?"

The twins looked at each other, and Marie said, "We aren't supposed to talk to summer people."

Henry said, "Come on! Don't call us summer people. We just came up here to visit Port Elizabeth and see what it is like. A fishing village is new to us, you know."

"We've been wanting to make friends with someone," said Benny, "but it's been very hard."

Then Marie spoke very fast. "Everybody said you were stuck-up, but I said you weren't. You aren't stuck-up at all! I was right! I know we haven't been very nice to you on this island, but Hal and I wondered. . . ."

"What did you wonder?" asked Benny. "I'd like to know."

The twins were quiet for a minute.

Then Marie said, "You see, we go to school in the winter. But the teachers don't like it here. They don't stay long. We had five teachers last year."

"Imagine having five teachers in one year!" said Benny.

"It's awful," said Hal. "Every new teacher thinks we have forgotten everything. So they all start back at the beginning."

"You don't get very far that way," said Henry.

"No," said Marie. "The last teacher told us to study this summer, but we don't know how. And we would love to learn to paint."

Jessie said, "Violet learned to paint in school. She loves it, too."

"Oh, would you teach us?" cried the twins.

"Of course," said Violet. "I'll do my best."

"Oh, thank you," said Marie, her eyes bright.

Hal said slowly, "We'd like to learn other things, too, but we don't know how."

Then Jessie woke up. Violet woke up. Henry woke up. As for Benny, he was already wide awake. They all saw what the twins really wanted.

Then the whole story came out. The Moss twins talked faster than ever.

Marie said, "The little children can't read, and they love stories. All the children in this village ought to go to school. Even the little ones would love it if you taught it. And all our mothers would be so glad."

"OK," said Benny. "So you want to go to summer school. Henry, let's teach school! Even I could teach. Just give me a few small kids, and I'll teach 'em to read. And I could teach singing. Now how about that old schoolhouse? That's empty, doing nothing."

"That belongs to Miss Elizabeth Gray," said Marie. "She has the key."

"Is she cross?" asked Benny. "Would she let us use the schoolhouse?"

"She might. She isn't cross, anyway. You could ask

her. I wouldn't dare," said Marie. "It would be grand if we could use the schoolhouse, wouldn't it?"

Henry began to climb down the rock. He said, "Never mind your painting this time, Violet. Let's go!"

"Oh, do you dare?" asked Hal.

"Why not?" said Benny. "She doesn't bite, does she?"

"No," said Hal, laughing a little. "But we won't go. You go."

Henry smiled. He said, "Yes, I guess four of us will be enough. We'll tell you later what she says."

Just then a loud whistle sounded. It whistled and whistled.

"That's for us!" cried Marie. "It's the sardine factory! A school of sardines has come in. Sardines have to be canned quick. We have to go. Please don't forget our school."

"No, we won't!" called Benny.

As they climbed down, Henry said to Jessie, "Remember my friend Larry in Adams College? He is going to live in a city this summer and help boys who live in a poor neighborhood catch up in school. Then they won't be drop-outs. And here we are on an island, doing about the same thing."

"I think it's an exciting idea," said Violet. "We didn't think we would be schoolteachers this summer, did we?"

"That's the last thing I thought of," said Henry. "Just look at everybody going to work."

Indeed somebody came out of every house. Sometimes there were three or four people from one house. They all hurried down to the factory.

"Well, well," said Jessie. "We have made friends at last."

"We made two, anyway," said Benny.

By that time Marie and Hal were almost out of sight.

CHAPTER 4

A Woman of Few Words

"Here we go, up to a strange mansion to see a strange lady," said Benny.

"Right!" said Henry. "I'm sure it's all right to ring a doorbell, even if we don't get in."

The four Aldens started along the beach, past the factory, and up the high cliff walk. They could see the mansion above them. It was a large square house, painted white. There was a square room on top that looked out to sea.

The Aldens climbed the steps to the front door and rang the bell. They could hear it ringing inside.

After a few minutes they heard someone coming very slowly. The door opened to show a tall, thin woman with straight gray hair. She did not smile. She just stood there.

Jessie began, "Miss Gray, I hope you will forgive us for coming to see you. But we are staying here for a while, and we want to ask you a favor."

Elizabeth Gray's eyes went sharply from one to another. Still she did not smile. Then she said shortly, "Come in." She stood aside for them to pass. "Go straight ahead," she said.

Benny thought, "Not a very warm welcome! Maybe we won't get that schoolhouse after all."

None of the Aldens knew that they were the first real callers Miss Gray had had for many years.

They all sat down. Miss Gray did not say a word. Henry found it hard to begin, but he knew he must say something. He began, "This is a funny question, Miss Gray. You see, we had no idea we would do this. But some of the children in Port Elizabeth want to go to school this summer to learn more. They asked us to help them. Maybe you think that is a queer idea."

"No," said Miss Gray, "I don't."

That was all she said. Still no smile.

Benny could not stand this. He said, "We came to ask you if we could use your schoolhouse. It's a wonderful schoolhouse! It has a big bell and everything. I'd be the one to ring the bell. Could we use it, do you think?"

"What would you do with it?"

Jessie answered this. She said, "We'd have a real school every morning, but we wouldn't use the schoolhouse at all in the afternoon."

Violet added, "We'd be very careful of it. We'd keep it clean, too."

"We'd always remember to lock the door," said Benny.

"No reason why you can't have it," said Miss Gray. "Certainly these children have never learned much."

"You are very kind," said Jessie. "We are strangers, and we have asked for a lot. I know that you are interested in the children. Everyone says so."

"Humph!" said Miss Gray.

Jessie went on, "We haven't told our grandfather yet. But I'm sure he will think this school is a good idea."

Benny laughed. He said, "Grandfather will think it is funny, though. *Me* teaching school!"

The sharp voice said, "What are you going to teach, boy?"

"Well, I don't know," said Benny. "Maybe I could teach them about the moon."

Miss Gray looked at Henry and said, "I'm sure they don't know much about the moon."

Benny said, "We didn't expect to teach school. We came up here to find a mystery."

"What? A mystery?" said Miss Gray. "Why?"

"Because my friend Max said we couldn't," said Benny. "He said this island was dull, and we couldn't have any adventure here."

Miss Gray said nothing. The Aldens had never met anyone before who talked so little and never smiled.

"Maybe we'd better go now," said Violet softly.

Miss Gray went stiffly over to a desk and took out two keys. "Back door, front door," she said. "They are marked." She gave the keys to Henry.

"We won't lose them," said Jessie. "We'll give them back to you when we go home."

"Give me your names," said Miss Gray. She picked up a small notebook from the table. Then the Aldens saw that a new book was lying on the table. The name of the book was *The Woman Who Talked Too Much*, by E. Gray.

They all thought E. Gray is Elizabeth Gray! She wrote that book. But she certainly doesn't talk much herself! But nobody dared to ask her any questions.

Jessie gave her the names.

"Your grandfather's name?"

Henry said, "He is James Henry Alden, and I'm Henry James Alden. We live in Greenfield."

Miss Gray had heard of the Alden Library in one town and the Alden Museum in another. But she did not say so.

Benny said, "Oh, Grandfather's wonderful! He's the best man you ever saw. We'll go and tell him right now that you are letting us use your schoolhouse."

The others wanted to go, so they were glad Benny had started toward the door. When they stood on the step they all said, "Goodbye! And thank you!"

Miss Gray did not say goodbye. Instead she called

suddenly, "Did you ever see a blond-haired man anywhere who smiles and shows his teeth all the time?"

"No, I'm sorry," began Henry.

"Don't be sorry," said Miss Gray sharply and shut the door.

"Well, what do you know!" said Benny, in a very low voice. "What does she mean by that?"

"I don't know," said Henry. "But keep your eyes open, Ben. Miss Gray doesn't ask questions for nothing."

The Aldens said no more until they were on the beach.

Then Benny said, "I don't think Miss Gray is really polite, but I suppose that's her way."

"We knew she was different," said Jessie. "That's why she lives all alone and never goes out. Maybe she doesn't like people."

Henry said, "We know she's a writer. Maybe she has to be alone. In a way I thought she liked the idea of the school, even if she didn't say so."

"Anyway, she gave us the schoolhouse," said Benny. "And that's why we went up there."

Then they walked as fast as they could to find Mr. Alden.

"Oh, Grandfather!" cried Benny when he saw a figure sitting in the sun by the hotel. "Please let us go to Northport this afternoon and buy paints and school things. We're going to teach school!"

"Teach school!" said Grandfather.

The young people tried not to talk all at once.

"We went up to ask Miss Gray—" began Benny.

"Oh, you did? I thought she didn't like visitors."

"Well, that's right, she doesn't. That's sure! But she gave us everything we asked for."

"Bless my soul! What did you ask for? From a perfect stranger!"

Henry looked straight at his grandfather and said, "It turned out very well, Grandfather. You see the red-haired twins asked us if we would help them with schoolwork. Just to catch up, you know. They said every child on the island would come. So that's why we wanted the schoolhouse."

"And she gave it to you?" asked Mr. Alden, laughing.

"Well, yes," said Jessie. "She doesn't talk much. But she must have liked the idea, really. She gave us the keys."

"She gave us a rough time, too," said Benny.

"Hard to talk to?" asked Mr. Alden.

"Very!" said Henry.

Benny said suddenly, "I'd like to forget Miss Gray. She is no fun at all. I'd rather think about our school. I'm going to ring that bell. And I'll ring it for recess, too."

Grandfather nodded. "Yes," he said. "I know how you feel, Benny. I never saw a bell rope myself without wanting to pull it." But he could see that his grandchildren had not received a very warm welcome from Miss Gray. He decided to talk with Henry later, when they were alone.

Violet said, "Grandfather, we think Marie and Hal Moss can paint. Wouldn't it be wonderful if they really could paint well?"

"Yes, my dear, it is a great thing to discover an artist. This school idea is a surprise to me, but it's fine. I never know what you will think of next!"

Henry said, "We thought we could go over to Northport and buy some paints and school things."

Mr. Alden laughed. "Yes," he said, "you can take the car. And maybe you will take me, too."

Everyone laughed at this. They always had a better time when Mr. Alden came along.

Thirty miles seemed a long drive because they wanted to get there and buy the things. They went first to a store to buy paints.

"Better get enough to go around," said Mr. Alden. "Give them a bit of fun. It isn't much fun with two sharing a paintbox."

In the end they bought ten boxes of paints. The older children could each have a box. They bought colored paper, small scissors, gold stars for Benny, and a stapler.

Jessie said, "Marie told us that there is plenty of chalk in the schoolroom closet. And there are pencils and paper left from last year, and some school books."

"Well," said Grandfather, "if you forget anything, we can come again. Let's eat supper at this little restaurant. It seems to be called the Sea Shell."

The Aldens noticed a bright red sports car parked in the yard. The top was down. "That car looks strange up here in such a quiet town," said Henry.

"It looks as if it goes fast," said Benny.

As they went into the Sea Shell a man with blond hair came out. He smiled at the Aldens and showed all his teeth. He said, "Hi, there!" although he was a perfect stranger. They watched him as he started the red car. Off he went like the wind.

"I told you that car could go fast," said Benny. "And wait! That man had blond hair, all right, and he smiled and showed all his teeth. There can't be two men like *him!* Just what Miss Gray said."

CHAPTER 5

The Money Man

When the Aldens drove back to the island they saw Hal and Marie waving to them from the beach. Marie shouted, "Please come over!"

"You go on," said Grandfather. "You don't need me."

The four Aldens ran down to the beach.

Hal said, "Guess who is coming to the island! The Money Man!"

Benny said, "The Money Man? Now who is that?"

Marie said, "Oh, he's a wonderful man who buys money. Pa had a quarter, and the Money Man gave him ten dollars for it."

"Whew, that's a lot of money!" said Benny. "How do you know he is coming again?"

"Somebody saw him in Northport and told Mr. Fenton," said Hal.

"Does he have blond hair?" asked Benny.

"Yes, he does, and white teeth," said Hal. "He has a big smile. He smiles at everybody."

"There you are, Jessie," said Henry with a nod.

Jessie said, "Yes, Mr. Fenton was right. You couldn't miss that man."

Marie said, "My pa says we ought to help you clean up the school. After all, it's for us. The big boys can help carry water, and there are more children to help if you want them."

"Good!" said Henry. "Let me see. We do need help, but it's too late to do anything now. Let's clean the school tomorrow morning and begin school the next day. That'll be Thursday."

"Funny day to begin school," said Benny. "But what do we care? We bought some paints and things in Northport."

"Let's meet at eight o'clock tomorrow morning at

the school," said Jessie. "Eight of us can do a lot of work."

As it turned out, there were more than eight. Several other children were waiting with Hal and Marie when the Aldens arrived the next morning.

Henry unlocked the front door, and they all went in and looked around.

"The room is dusty," said Marie.

It was an old-fashioned schoolroom. The desks and seats were fastened to the floor.

"I'd like my children in the front row," said Benny. "Your big children can sit in the back seats."

This was really the only way, because the front seats were small and the back seats were large.

Henry set everyone to work. The children took the books off the shelves and washed the shelves. Every book was dusted and set back. The children were delighted with their own work. The biggest boys washed the seats and desks. The teacher's desk was washed, and a new pink blotter put in the middle.

"Will somebody bring flowers for this desk tomorrow?" asked Jessie.

"Oh, I will!" cried a child named Isabelle. "We have a big vine of pink roses all over our roof."

There was a wood stove in the back of the room and a woodbox. Hal wiped off the stove. Then he said, "How about the woodbox? It looks all right to me."

Henry agreed. "Just brush off the top. We certainly won't have a fire. Leave the wood for winter."

A little later Benny was standing still, looking at a big picture on the wall. It hung in the front of the room where the big chimney was. He said, "Look at this picture of George Washington. White wig and hair ribbon and all! What can we do about that? It looks dark and dirty."

The painting showed the first President in his old-fashioned costume, standing beside a table.

"You can't clean that, Benny," said Violet. "It would spoil it to wash it. And it's too high, anyway."

"Just let it alone, huh?" said Benny. "I'm glad we don't have to wear fancy clothes like that with all those buttons down the coat."

"So am I," said Jimmy. "I've got to go home now, Mr. Benny."

"Don't call me Mr. Benny. I'm not really a teacher. Why do you have to go home?"

"I've got to find some old bottles out in the fish house," said Jimmy. "The Money Man wants 'em. I've got to have them all ready."

"Yes," agreed his sister. "He even wants an old olive bottle! I've found that already. It says Queen Olives, 1875, on it. Ma says her ma must have bought it. Isn't he a funny man? To want an old dusty bottle almost a hundred years old?" Then she added quickly, "But he's wonderful just the same."

All the children were listening now. They nodded their heads. An older boy named Jeffrey Frost said, "My pa and ma have been waiting for the Money Man to come. He told them to find all the funny old things they could. He likes 'em! Ma found an old glass pitcher and a whale's tooth with pictures on it."

Henry said, "Jeffrey, do you know where that whale's tooth came from?"

"Oh, yes, my great uncle made the pictures when he sailed on an old whaling ship. That tooth is so heavy you wouldn't believe it!"

Jessie said, "Well, we've finished our work here, anyway. We'll all go home now and start school tomorrow."

"What time does school begin?" asked Jeffrey.

"Nine o'clock," said Henry. "You'll hear the bell."

"I'm going to ring the bell," added Benny.

"That's lots of fun," said Jimmy.

"Maybe you can be the bell ringer later," said Benny. "Tell all the other children, won't you?"

"Tell them?" said Marie, laughing. "Most of the children are here now. The rest will know just as soon as we get home."

"No school in the afternoon?" asked Jeffrey.

"No, I'm sorry," said Henry. "You ought to help at home."

"I suppose so," said Marie. Then her face lighted up and she said, "I'm going to clean up my room just like this schoolroom. My sister will help me. She sleeps there, too."

The schoolroom was indeed clean. Henry locked the door, and the children ran off in all directions.

The Aldens found Grandfather waiting for lunch. When they were sitting down at the table, Henry said, "We are worried, Grandfather, about the Money Man. I'm afraid he is cheating everyone on the island."

"I'm sure he is," said Jessie. "You see, he paid ten dollars for an old quarter. That made them all trust him. But who knows? That quarter may be worth a hundred dollars."

"Or a thousand!" said Benny. "You see, Grandfather, there really is a mystery here. I don't think the Money Man is as wonderful as he seems."

Grandfather smiled. "Well, Benny," he said, "I'm sure you will keep your eyes open. If this man goes too far, we'll try to stop him. But I agree with you. He isn't wonderful at all!"

CHAPTER 6

Mystery Painting

It was a wonderful moment when Benny rang the school bell. Dingdong! Dingdong! Everyone on the island heard it and smiled. Benny did not really need to ring the bell at all—because every child was already in the school yard.

The girls and boys rushed in. They could hardly wait to see what was going to happen. They had no idea what their four young teachers would do.

"Here's my seat," cried Isabelle. "I sat here last year. And here are the pink roses."

All of Benny's class rushed up to the small front seats. The big boys and girls sat down in the back seats.

And the middle-sized ones sat in the middle. There were twenty children when Benny counted them.

Henry began to talk. The children were suddenly very quiet. He said, "Today we will have four classes. First you tell us what grade you were in last year. Now, who was in Isabelle's class? You stand up, and Benny will see how many there are."

"Don't we call him Mr. Benny?" asked Isabelle.

"No," said Benny, "just call me Benny. And don't ever call me Teacher."

"I always call my teachers Teacher," said Isabelle.

Benny laughed. "I guess you are going to be my talker. There's always a talker in every class."

Soon Jessie said, "We will have a spelling match today and a singing school and a new game at recess."

"Ah!" whispered the children. They were all smiles. School had never been like this.

There were five children in Benny's class and five in Violet's, six in Jessie's, and four in Henry's. Henry said, "Sometimes we will change teachers. Now we will write down your names and get started."

Benny sat down with his class and took all their

names. Then he said, "Isabelle, you let somebody else tell me what book you can read."

Tommy Spoon said, "We can't read any book. The teacher took the books with her."

Benny was all ready for this. He had not found any easy books on the shelf.

"I'll write on the board," he said. He printed in big letters, "I have a dog."

"I have a dog," said Tommy Spoon. "That's what it says."

"Right!" said Benny. "You read it, Eddie." Eddie was the smallest child.

"No," said Eddie, shaking his head, "no dog."

"You mean you haven't any dog?" asked Benny. "Well, can't you read it, even if you haven't any dog?"

"No," said Eddie crossly. "No dog!"

"Well," said Benny, laughing, "have you a cat?"

Yes, Eddie had a cat. So Benny printed, "I have a cat." Eddie read it very well. "I know *cat* is the last word. My cat's name is Fish."

"Fish!" said Benny. "Why?"

"Because he always comes when we call 'Fish, Fish.' "

Benny printed the whole story. They all read it together.

I have a cat.
His name is Fish.
I call, "Fish, Fish."
Fish comes.

"Oh, I like to read about myself!" said Eddie.

Then Benny saw that he would have to make his own reading books. While the children were busy making figure 2's, Benny printed the story about Eddie's cat five times on paper. Every child could read it. Benny said they could take the story home.

"Write about me next time," begged Isabelle. "I've got a boat."

"So have I," said every child.

"We'll all read about Isabelle's boat tomorrow," said Benny.

The older children had books. They even had spelling books. After reading and a spelling match, Henry said, "Now we will have an art lesson all

together. Let's study that painting of George Washington."

As Henry pointed out the different things in the picture, Benny was interested.

Henry went on, "You may think it is strange that a strong man would wear ruffles. But every well-dressed gentleman wore short knee pants and long white stockings and shoes with buckles. And now look at the hair. What color is it?"

"White!" shouted every child.

"Yes, it is white. But it is a wig. This is a very good painting, you see. That wig looks exactly like hair."

Jessie said, "Now notice the eyes. George Washington seems to be looking right at you. It takes a fine artist to do that."

Everyone looked at the eyes. All but Benny. He happened to look at the coat buttons. There was a long row of buttons down the right side of Washington's velvet coat.

Benny thought, "One of those buttons looks awfully strange to me. It looks like a round hole instead of a button."

He couldn't very well tell Henry, so he wisely said nothing. After the art lesson, Henry said, "Now ring the bell for recess, Ben."

"Recess!" said Jimmy. "It can't be time for recess."

But it was. Time had gone fast for all the children.

"Come outdoors, and we'll teach you a new game," said Jessie.

The children made a circle and had already played the game once when they heard a car. They all looked, and a bright red sports car came bumping over the rocky road to the island. It was low tide. The game stopped.

The children called out, "Oh, oh! Look, there's the Money Man!"

A man put his head out of the car window and waved and smiled. He called "Hello! Hello, kids!" But he did not stop.

When he had gone, Benny said, "Tell me about this Money Man, Isabelle."

"Oh, he gives us things. He came down here last year. You ought to see the big doll he gave me!"

"Why did he give you a doll?" asked Henry.

"He traded it for my old one," said Isabelle. "I had a teeny little wooden doll only this long." She showed with her small hands. "My grandfather made it with his knife. And the man said if I'd trade, he'd give me a beautiful doll with a pink silk dress. And he did."

"Money Man isn't his name," said Hal. "We just call him that. His name is Mr. Fred Willet."

Marie showed Jessie a chain of bright red beads she had around her neck. "The man gave me this, too," she said.

"And what did you trade it for?" asked Violet.

"Oh, you'd laugh! It was a string of old buttons. Ma said I could string the buttons and wear them for a necklace. They were old things anyway. Ma said most of them were on her grandmother's dresses. You can see they were old."

Henry looked at Jessie. Then he said, "Why do you think he is here again? To trade?"

"Oh, I hope so," said Eddie. "I've got an old iron bank. You put in a penny and a little man comes out and goes back in. The Money Man said I could have a real watch for it or a new cap. I couldn't decide then. But I know now. I want the watch."

Then the game went on. Benny knew that something was wrong. He saw Henry whisper to Jessie, "I wish we could get word to Grandfather that the Money Man has arrived."

Violet heard this, too. She whispered to Henry, "Don't worry. Grandfather's eyes are wide open. And he doesn't miss much."

Then it was time to go in for the singing school.

Jessie taught the children a new song. It was a round with three parts.

Right after the song, the sardine factory whistle blew. Everybody except the Aldens ran.

Benny went up to look at the picture of George Washington again. He said softly to Henry, "Don't go yet. Wait till the children are out of sight."

When the last one had shouted goodbye, Benny took his family up to the front of the room to look at Washington. "Look at button number five," he said. "There's a hole in the picture. The fifth button *is* a hole."

"Why, so it is!" cried Jessie. "I wonder why."

"I wonder what is behind it," said Violet.

"The back hall," said Henry.

They all went into the tiny back hall. The back door was there with a window beside it. The huge chimney made one wall of the room. There was a big pile of wood.

"We haven't time to look around any more," said Jessie. "I'm worried about that Mr. Willet. He's here now. I wish Grandfather could stop him before he cheats any more people."

Jessie did not need to worry so much. The Money Man had gone from the schoolhouse straight to Mr. Fenton's store. When he went in, there was Grandfather leaning on the counter, drinking a cup of coffee.

CHAPTER 7

Grandfather Makes a Call

The Money Man was not at all shy when he saw Mr. Alden. He said brightly, "I'm Freddy Willet, at your service. Introduce me, Fenton, to your friend. I'm a coin dealer. A few antiques, too. Call me Freddy."

Mr. Alden nodded and said, "How do you do, Mr. Willet. So you're a coin dealer?"

"Yes, sir! And let me tell you, the people on this island save everything. Never throw anything away. It's a great place."

"Really?" said Mr. Alden. "Will these people sell you their things?"

"Sure. They have a lot of old money tucked away. It came from their great-grandfathers, I guess. They trust me because I gave one of them ten dollars for an old quarter. Who wouldn't take ten dollars for a quarter?"

Mr. Alden wanted to say "I wouldn't," but he said nothing. He went on drinking coffee.

Mr. Willet looked at Mr. Alden's watch chain. He said, "Do you mind if I look? That big old penny on your chain—do you know what that's worth?"

"Well," said Grandfather, "not much, I guess."

"You're dead right," said Mr. Willet. "It's got that hole in it, so it isn't worth anything at all. But if some idiot hadn't made that hole it would be worth two hundred and fifty dollars. Yes, sir, no fooling! It's very rare."

Mr. Alden said, "Yes, I know. That's why I wear it. I was the idiot who made that hole."

"Sorry!" said Mr. Willet with a wink. "Didn't mean to hurt your feelings. By the way, have you any coins on you? I just take a quick look and I know."

Mr. Alden emptied his pockets on the counter. Mr.

Willet quickly turned each piece of money over to see the date.

"No." He shook his head. "Nothing there."

"How about this?" Mr. Alden took an old dime from his vest pocket.

Freddy took one look and said, "Ah!" Then he took a magnifying glass from his pocket and held it over the dime.

At last he looked up and said slowly, "Mr. A., you have a rare dime here. I'll be glad to buy it for a hundred dollars. And *cash*."

Mr. Alden shook his head again. "No, I ought to have told you it is not for sale. I just wanted to know how much it was worth."

"Well, now you know," said Freddy. "Sure you don't want to sell it?"

"Sure," said Mr. Alden.

This did not stop Mr. Willet. He went on, "I sell coins to fine places. To colleges and museums. Other things, too. I know people who would be delighted to get that dime."

But Mr. Alden still said no. He looked at his watch.

Mr. Willet went closer to Mr. Alden. He said in a low voice, "Listen, Mr. A., you seem to be a nice sort of chap. That watch of yours is very old. I collect things like that. I'll give you a beautiful modern watch for that watch. I bet it doesn't keep very good time."

"It keeps excellent time," said Mr. Alden. "I don't want to sell it or trade it."

"Well," said Mr. Willet brightly, "maybe you'll change your mind. I'll be around." He winked and went out of the store.

Grandfather watched Freddy from the door. "Now I do hope he won't go up and try to buy anything from Miss Elizabeth Gray," he said.

"Oh, he won't!" said Mr. Fenton. "He'll never get in there. The maid Eva sees to that. She doesn't let anyone in."

"I see," said Grandfather. "By the way, what is the matter with Miss Gray? Why does she keep herself shut up in that house?"

"I don't really know," said Mr. Fenton. "She's always been that way. She is almost a hermit. All I know is that she hardly ever comes out of her house."

"She must care about the children of the island if she lets them use the schoolhouse this summer."

"Yes, I suppose so," said Mr. Fenton. "Here's another thing. Have you seen that little white building on one side of my store? Well, that's the Gray Library. Miss Gray's grandfather was a book collector. Miss Gray built that library and gave a lot of her grandfather's books to the island people. But nobody ever goes there."

"Why not?"

"Well, the books aren't interesting," said Mr. Fenton. "They are all old fashioned and in fine print. Nobody can read 'em."

"How do you get in?" asked Mr. Alden.

"Walk in!" said Mr. Fenton, laughing. "It's never locked. A young girl used to stay there on Saturdays, but she just sat there. Nobody came. So she doesn't come any more, and the library's always empty."

Mr. Alden was thinking it very strange that the island people didn't know who Miss Gray was. They did not know that she was a famous author. Long before the Aldens had come to the island, Grandfather had read all her books. He knew that she was well known for her help to many schools all over the country.

"That's too bad," said Mr. Alden. "Probably they are all good books." But then he changed the subject, asking, "What do you think of Freddy?"

"I don't like him," said Mr. Fenton at once. "He may be a coin dealer, but he's something else, too. I don't trust him."

"I wonder why these island people trust him?" said Mr. Alden.

"Oh, that's easy. That ten dollar bill he gave to Moss for an old quarter, that did it! Nobody had ever heard of such a thing. I tried to tell them, but they wouldn't listen."

Grandfather said, "I think I'll go up to Miss Gray's and see if I get in."

"You will," said Mr. Fenton. "Eva will know you should be let in."

Mr. Alden nodded. "But first I think I had better call up a friend of mine. Could I use your telephone?"

There was a telephone on the wall near the door.

"Go right ahead," Mr. Fenton said. "I have to step out just now."

Mr. Alden's call was short, but he seemed pleased. He walked up to the mansion. He took off his hat and rang the bell. Eva knew who he was the minute she saw him through the curtain.

She opened the door and said, "You are Mr. Alden. Miss Gray will see you."

Mr. Alden followed Eva into the parlor. "It's Mr. Alden," said Eva.

Miss Gray was sitting at her desk with her back to the door. She turned around and said, "Sit down, please."

Grandfather drew a chair nearer to Miss Gray and said, "You have been very kind to my grandchildren. I want to thank you. I can't stay long because they will miss me and wonder where I am. But before I go, I want to tell you that a queer-acting coin dealer is loose on this island."

Miss Gray rapped on her desk with a pencil. Then she said sharply, "Freddy Willet!"

"I see you know his name. I just wanted you to know what was going on. I think he plans to cheat these island people this time. Then they'll never see him again."

There was a pause, then Miss Gray said, "Thank you very much."

CHAPTER 8

Caught by the Tide

When Mr. Alden met his grandchildren at noon they were all bursting with news. Mr. Alden certainly had news, too, but he did not tell it then. Nobody thought of lunch. They were too busy talking.

Henry was the one to tell his grandfather about the toy bank and the old wooden doll and the string of buttons. He said, "This man is cheating the people in two ways. First he doesn't pay enough for the old coins, and then he trades their treasures for cheap things. The new things are bright colored, so the children are delighted. They haven't any idea that old buttons are worth anything."

Benny added, "Of course my little Isabelle thinks her new doll is lots better than an old wooden doll. It really is prettier."

Grandfather nodded and said, "This Mr. Willet is certainly not honest. I'm sure of that. Those old iron banks are worth much more than a knife."

Henry said, "Freddy is clever. So far he hasn't done a thing that is against the law. The people here think he pays enough. They are delighted to trade."

"So he hasn't really stolen a thing," finished Benny.

"Exactly right! You just wait," said Jessie. "He will go from one house to another. But even if he should steal things, what can we do, Grandfather?"

Mr. Alden said, "You children can't arrest him, certainly." They all laughed at the idea.

Then they began to tell Mr. Alden about school. He watched Jessie and Violet. They looked tired to him. He said, "Let's have another quick lunch today. Then we can eat an early supper at the Sea Shell. You girls look tired."

"Oh, no, we're not tired!" Jessie said. "We are just thinking hard."

But both girls were willing to set out the peanut butter and jelly for sandwiches and have doughnuts and milk for dessert. Then the four teachers began to study their lessons for the next day.

"It's a funny feeling," said Mr. Alden, "to see you all sitting around doing schoolwork in vacation."

"This doesn't seem like work," said Violet. "It's just something very interesting mixed up with a thief and a poor rich lady living all alone."

"And lots of cute children," said Benny. "Anyway, I can tell Max that something happened on his old island—but I'm not quite sure what it is yet."

The Aldens sat out in the yard by their hotel with their work. From there they could see the store and the beach and the houses. They could see everything in the village except the mansion. But nobody saw Freddy Willet. The afternoon passed quickly.

Then about five o'clock they saw the red car go bumping over the rocky road to Northport.

Mr. Alden got up and took his hat. "I have an idea," he said. "Let's go right now to the Sea Shell and have supper."

"Right!" said Henry. He went at once to get the car. They all thought that Grandfather was following Freddy, but they did not say so.

When Henry drove into the parking place of the Sea Shell, there was the red sports car!

"I wonder why the Money Man comes over here to eat," said Benny.

"He has to," said Henry. "There's no place to eat on the island."

Sure enough, there was the Money Man sitting at a table with two other people, a man and a woman. He said to the Aldens "Hello, there," and went right on talking to his guests.

Suddenly Henry whispered to Benny, "Change seats with me, Ben, will you?" Benny got up at once without asking why. He knew that Henry would tell him later. Now Henry sat with his back to the other table. Grandfather himself wondered why.

When their waitress had left them, Henry said in a low voice, "I know those people with Mr. Willet. The man is Dr. James English. He runs the museum at Adams College, and the woman is Miss Cox, the librarian. I hope they won't see me."

"I bet Freddy is trying to sell them something," whispered Benny.

Grandfather said, "That's just what he's doing. I'm sure of it."

"How do you know?" whispered Benny.

"I've met him," said Grandfather. "I met him this morning in the store. He tried to buy my watch and the big penny on my watch chain."

"Oh, you'd never sell those! Mr. Willet picked the wrong man that time," Benny said. "Nobody could cheat you, Grandfather."

Mr. Alden laughed quietly. He was watching Mr. Willet out of the corner of his eye. But he didn't see

him give anything to the strangers. Suddenly he said, "Let's get out of here before Freddy gets through with his dinner. We don't want his friends to see Henry."

This was easy. Mr. Willet and his friends had just started on their dinner, and they were eating very slowly. The Aldens just went without dessert. When they left the table, they all stood behind Henry to cover him up. Henry went out at once to the car on the other side of the parking lot, and Mr. Alden waited to pay the bill.

Freddy Willet looked up and saw Mr. Alden.

The Aldens sat in the car for a few minutes. "What do you think Freddy is going to do, Grandfather?" asked Benny.

"That's what I wanted to find out. He saw me, but he didn't speak," said Mr. Alden. "I think he's making a deal with Adams College. I hope he won't fool the librarian."

Henry said, "She's pretty smart, and she would know what coins are worth."

He started the car and turned into the road.

The drive of thirty miles seemed longer than ever. As they came near the island, Violet was looking ahead. "Oh, look, Henry! The tide!"

"Oh, dear," said Jessie. "The tide has turned! Why didn't we think of that? It's getting dark, too."

Henry stopped the car and they all looked ahead. There was no road to the island. It was covered with seawater, which was getting deeper every minute.

"I don't dare try it, Grandfather," said Henry, frowning.

"Right, my boy! If we got stuck half way over, it would be no fun, I can tell you."

Henry said, "I thought it seemed awfully wet when we came over. But I knew you must be following Freddy, and I don't think he gets caught like this very often."

"By the way," cried Benny, "I wonder what Freddy will do? He'll be caught, too. It will be six hours before it's low tide again."

"It will be nearer twelve hours, Ben," said Henry. "You see the tide hasn't been coming in long."

"Let's see," said Jessie. "It is about eight o'clock

now. The tide will be high at midnight, and low again at six o'clock in the morning!"

"We're not in any danger, though, are we, Grandfather?" said Violet.

"No, my dear. We will just have to find a place to sleep."

"Oh, boy!" shouted Benny. "We could sleep in the car! That's what this station wagon is made for. We could do it, Grandfather!"

"Five people?" asked Grandfather, smiling.

Benny said, "I could take the car blanket and sleep on the top of the car. Oh, please!"

Grandfather laughed. He said, "I don't think we would get much sleep. But I suppose you young people don't mind that."

"I don't," said Jessie. "I'd like to wait and see what Freddy will do."

"Very well," said Grandfather. "Find a place off the road, Henry, and we'll try it."

CHAPTER 9

The Disappearing Stranger

Henry backed the car into the woods a little way. Nobody could see it from the road. The Aldens all got out and took out every car rug that they could find for bedclothes. It was so warm that they didn't really need any covers.

Henry and Benny let down the seats that made beds for four people. By nine o'clock all was ready. Benny climbed up on top of the car.

"I won't fall down," he called. "There's a railing all around the edge. I'm going to put this blanket under me instead of over me." He folded the car blanket and lay down. "A very soft bed," he said.

"I should think Freddy would be along soon—if he's coming," said Jessie. "I wonder what he will do."

In about an hour they heard a car coming. It did not make much noise, but everyone was awake. Benny sat up and looked through the trees. "Yes, it's a car," he whispered.

But the car stopped. Everyone was watching it now. Mr. Freddy must have seen that the tide was in, because he quietly turned his car around and went back.

"Now what?" Benny whispered down. "I don't think he is going to give up like that. He would just love to be on the island when we are away. He knows we are watching him, I bet."

They all lay down again. But nobody went to sleep. It was not too long before they heard another very soft sound. It sounded like water, and it was ahead of them. They all looked hard through the darkness.

"He's got a boat!" whispered Henry. They all watched. Then they all saw it. It was a rowboat with Mr. Willet's head showing against the dark sky.

"Come down now, Benny," whispered Grandfather. "We'll get a boat, too!"

"Oh, can we really?" whispered Benny. "Where can we get a boat?"

"Where Mr. Willet got his, I think," said Grandfather.

They all sat up in the car, and Henry drove back over the road very carefully.

"There's a light!" said Violet. "It's in a fisherman's hut."

Henry stopped the car in front of the house.

"Somebody is awake," said Jessie. "And do I see the end of that red car sticking out behind the house?"

"You do," said Mr. Alden. "I do, anyway. I think this is the place where Freddy got his boat. You do the talking, Henry."

Henry went to the door and knocked. At once a fisherman came to the door. He wore an old coat.

"I'm sorry to come so late," began Henry, "but we need a boat. It's high tide, and we're stuck."

"Yep, I know that," said the man. "Seems as if everybody is stuck tonight on the wrong side."

"Can we rent a boat from you?" asked Henry.

"Sure! I've got three. I just rented two."

"Two!" said Henry in surprise.

"Yep, two. One man came, and then another man came. You can have the last one."

"Where is it?" asked Henry.

"It's tied down near the road, when there is a road. You'll see it on the bank on the left, tied to a post. Can't miss it."

"How much will it be?" asked Henry. He couldn't help wondering about two men. He had been thinking only of Freddy Willet.

"A dollar," said the man. "Be sure and tie her up on the island side. My boys can row 'em back tomorrow. It ain't far."

Henry quickly gave the man a dollar and thanked him. Then he went back to the family. He said, "Do you suppose five of us can get into one boat?"

"We'll see," said Grandfather. "I think so."

Benny had heard about the two men. He could hardly wait to speak. "Who do you suppose that other man was? A mystery, for sure."

Mr. Alden was thinking, too. "I wonder," he said.

Henry drove back to the water. Sure enough, a boat was tied up on the bank.

"Good! It's a big one," said Grandfather. "I wonder why we didn't see it. Back the car off the road again, Henry. I guess this night's sleep is over."

Everybody got out of the car and went carefully down to the boat. When Henry came, they all pushed the boat into the water. Henry helped Violet and Jessie into the front of the boat, and Benny stepped into the other end. When Grandfather was sitting down on the middle seat, Henry pushed off. He and his grandfather began to row.

"We'll tie up just below the schoolhouse," said Henry. "I suppose we will see the other two boats there."

It was not very far to the island, but it was dark, and the tide was very high. They could see a little through the darkness. But there were no boats to be seen!

"What do you know!" said Benny. "Where would Freddy go? Do you think he has a partner, Grandfather?"

"Well," said Mr. Alden, "I don't know. If the man is a partner of Willet's, why would he come by himself?"

"That's so," Jessie said.

Benny added, "But I'm almost sure the first man must have crossed over to the island before we came. We were watching and listening all the time."

Henry ran the boat up on the beach. He tied it to a tree.

Suddenly Violet looked around and asked, "Where do you suppose Freddy has gone?" She shivered a little.

"Not to the hotel," Jessie said. "And I don't think he would stay with any of the island people."

"I wonder," said Henry. "I just wonder—"

"I know," said Benny. "The schoolhouse!"

Benny would have run to peek in the windows, but Grandfather said, "How do you know that Freddy isn't going back to the other side after getting something? The best thing we can do now is to get some sleep."

"And there's school tomorrow," said Violet.

CHAPTER 10

A Discovery

At breakfast they talked about the two boats and the two men.

"It's time to ring the bell," said Benny. "I have to go."

But Benny really had something else in mind. He wanted to look around the schoolhouse. He wanted to see where the hole went in George Washington's coat button.

Benny unlocked the schoolroom door and went at once into the back hall. The wood for the winter was there, piled high. There was the back door, a window, and the big chimney. He rattled the window. It was unlocked. The lock was very old and looked as if it hadn't been locked for a long time. Benny tried it. The lock was broken. It certainly had been broken for years.

Benny looked at the floor under the window and saw some flakes of dry white paint just exactly like the dry paint on the windowsill.

"I bet someone came through this window last night," he thought. "But why? I like to do things by myself, but this time I wish I could tell John Carter who works for Grandfather. After all, he used to be an F.B.I. man."

Benny looked around again. Only the big chimney was left, and the broom closet next to it. He opened the small door. Just a broom closet. There was a broom in it.

At recess Benny got word to his family to wait after the children had gone home at noon. When they were alone in the school yard, Jessie said, "Well, Benny, what's all this?"

"The back hall," said Benny. "Come and see."

The four Aldens all went into the tiny back hall.

"See that old dry paint on the floor?" said Benny.

"Yes, old man," said Henry. He bent over to look. "You are clever! This hasn't been here long. Somebody must have come in through the window. Maybe this is where Freddy slept last night."

"This broom closet is just a broom closet," said Benny. He opened the door beside the huge chimney. "See, there's a broom in it."

"Wait!" said Henry. "See those wood planks this closet is made of? If we could only pry them off—"

Henry opened his knife and pried away at one board. It was loose and came off easily. And there was a little brick room in the chimney!

"I thought this chimney was awfully big," said Henry. "And it has a queer shape. This is the reason, of course. Somebody wanted to make a place to hide in."

"Who?" asked Benny.

"Well, I don't know. It was made that way when the schoolhouse was built, and that was a long time ago. I do know that a lot of New England people built their houses with a hiding place in the chimney. I'm sure this is one of them. A perfect place!"

"It is a perfect place for us, too," said Benny, "if we want to watch what is going on in the schoolroom."

"What's the idea, Benny?" asked Violet. "Why would we ever want to watch the children?"

"Not the children, Violet!" said Benny. "Not in the daytime, either. At night! We can watch Freddy Willet if he ever comes in here, and I think he does."

"I think so, too, Ben," said Henry. "He must have some place to hide his things."

They put the planks back, locked the front door, and went home to lunch. They told Mr. Alden all about the room in the chimney. After lunch, Grandfather said, "I know something you don't know!"

The children laughed. "What is it?" asked Violet.

Then Mr. Alden told them about the Gray Library and the old books. When Benny heard it, he pushed back his bench. "That's where I'm going," he said. "Maybe I can find some pictures for my class."

"I don't think you will, Benny," said Mr. Alden. "Mr. Fenton said the books were all old."

"Well, maybe there's an old picture of George

Washington," said Benny. "Anyway I want to see the library."

Benny took a notebook, and off he went. Sure enough, the door of the library was not locked. Benny gave it a push and went right in. He found himself in a room just the size of the building. There were bookcases all around the room and one tall one down the middle.

"Well, here goes!" said Benny out loud. He began to whistle. He went to the first bookcase. He looked at the dusty books on the top shelves. Then he dropped to his knees to look at the books near the floor. All at once he had a queer feeling that someone was in the room. He listened, but he didn't hear a sound.

"This is nonsense," he thought. "Mr. Fenton says nobody ever comes here."

Then he heard a very, very soft noise. "What is that?" he thought. "Somebody is certainly in here!" But he did not get up or turn around. He listened. Then he heard the noise again. It was behind the middle bookcase. Benny knew that he couldn't see over it if he did turn around. Then there was a soft thud and then another. Benny rushed around the bookcase just in time to see the fingers of a hand disappear from the sill of the open window.

"Well, well, Mr. Willet!" said Benny out loud. He rushed to the window and looked out. Nobody was in sight.

"Freddy is hiding, that's sure," said Benny to himself. "He hasn't had time to get anywhere. But I know what I'm going to do." He ran up the cliff walk to the mansion!

Benny smiled as he rang the bell because he saw Eva peeking at him. In a minute Miss Gray herself opened the door.

"Sorry, Miss Gray," said Benny, very fast, "I think someone just stole some books out of the library. I thought I ought to tell you first. Maybe those books are valuable."

Eva's eyes grew big and round as Miss Gray said, "Thank you, Benny. I'll look myself. Nobody else knows the books. You come, too, Eva."

The three people went quickly down the cliff. Miss Gray went into the library and straight over to the last rows of books. There was the empty space exactly where she thought it would be. She knew which were the most valuable books, and so did Mr. Willet.

"There are four books gone here," she said. "They were a set. I never had an idea they would be stolen. And over here! Yes, some more are missing. Mr. Willet must have been here before."

She went around the room and found empty spaces everywhere. "Oh, dear!" said Miss Gray. "He has taken the very best books! He can sell them for a lot of money."

"But look here, Miss Gray," said Benny. "See this sign? It says you can borrow anything you want and sign your name. And here is Freddy Willet's name!"

"I don't think he will bring them back," said Miss Gray. "How foolish I was not to lock the door!"

"I don't think so," said Benny. "Freddy would have climbed in the window. Windows and doors don't stop our Freddy. That's why I think he is a thief. Don't worry too much, Miss Gray. My grandfather has Freddy on his mind. And my grandfather doesn't slip up very often."

CHAPTER 11

Who Is the Englishman?

Benny went slowly back to the hotel. He looked on every side as he walked, but Mr. Willet had disappeared.

Benny did some hard thinking on that walk. He had been sure that Freddy Willet was going to do more trading. But as far as Benny could tell, the Aldens and Miss Gray were the only people who knew Freddy was on the island today. After all, he hadn't come in his red sports car. He had come secretly in the middle of the night. Why?

One idea came to Benny. Freddy had planned to get the library books on this day while the Aldens were still busy with their school. It was just bad luck for Freddy that Benny had gone to the library to hunt for pictures.

When he reached home, Benny told the family about his adventures. Henry said, "Ben, you certainly have made a friend of Miss Gray. I thought you could. Why, you have even made her come out of her house."

Jessie said, "We've been here in the yard, but we haven't seen Mr. Willet or anyone new."

Mr. Alden said, "It's a mystery how two men can keep themselves out of sight. This is such a small place."

Nothing else happened that day. Everything seemed peaceful—too peaceful, the Aldens thought.

The next day was Saturday. The first thing the Aldens saw in the morning was children fishing. The island children sat on the edge of the wharf with long fishlines. They did not need poles.

Grandfather said, "Let's go fishing!"

"Fine," said Jessie. "We can watch the whole island from the wharf."

In a short time the whole family was sitting on the edge of the wharf with the children. Mr. Alden gave Hal a dollar for five fishlines. Eddie said, "I'll show you how to fish, Mr. Alden. You let the line way down. Then pull it up just a little and let it down again. Keep the hook wiggling."

The Aldens did as Eddie said. The island children were catching fish after fish. But the Aldens caught nothing. Suddenly Mr. Alden had a bite.

"Pull her in, mister!" cried Eddie. "Don't rush it. Hand over hand! But keep it even-like."

Mr. Alden pulled as well as he could through thirty feet of water, and landed a beautiful big fish on the wharf.

Benny said, "Aren't you going to fish any more, Grandfather?"

"No. I'm afraid I'll catch another."

"Well, I'm not," said Benny. "I wish I could catch one. I would eat that whole fish myself."

Everyone was quiet. The island children went on pulling in the fish. But the Aldens still caught nothing.

All at once Grandfather said slowly, "I believe I see our strange man at last!" Something in Grandfather's voice made the Aldens look up quickly at the cliff walk. The island children paid no attention.

"Who in the world is that?" said Jessie. "He is dressed like an Englishman."

The stranger wore a cap that shaded his eyes. He had on dark blue shorts and a soft shirt with a scarf tucked in at the neck. His socks were red and blue and came up to his knees. He carried a walking stick.

"Maybe he's a friend of Miss Gray's," said Henry. "He is coming from that way."

Then Violet said in a very low voice, "Grandfather! Do look at him! It's Mr. Carter!"

"It is," said Henry softly. "Look at his walk! It's John Carter's walk. Now why is he here?"

Mr. Alden said, "I telephoned him about Willet, but I didn't send for him. Maybe he began to look up Willet's business and thinks we need help."

Henry whispered, "He's coming this way. Act as if you don't know him."

The man in shorts came down to the wharf. Benny

wanted to smile, but he stopped in time.

"Hello, everybody! Fishing?" said the man, as if he had never seen the Aldens before.

"Well, sir, these children are fishing," said Mr. Alden. "But we have caught only one."

"I say, that's a big one!" It was exactly as if an Englishman were speaking. Not one of the island children turned around. But they heard every word.

"You're a stranger here, sir," said Grandfather. "Are you staying long?"

"A week or so, don't you know? My name is Wilder-Smith. Guest of Miss Gray's. My mother went to college with Miss Gray. Great old friends."

"We are the Aldens," said Grandfather. "Henry, Jessie, Violet, and Benny."

Mr. Wilder-Smith bowed. He knew that the island children were listening. He went on, "There's another stranger here, Mr. Willet. Today he is going to visit the good people and look over some dusty old things. He likes old things. Bit odd, don't you know?"

Isabelle spoke up loudly. "He isn't odd. He's wonderful!"

"There, now," said Mr. Wilder-Smith, "you see! He's wonderful. I may go with Mr. Willet on his calls."

"Go with him?" asked Benny, surprised.

"The man invited me. Of course I don't know anything about old things. By the way, did you know there is no post office on this island?"

"Yes, the mail has to come from Northport," said Henry.

Mr. Wilder-Smith shook his head. "I'll have to find some other way. I have to get my letters by fast post."

"Maybe we can think of a way to help you," said Benny. "We've got a car."

"Right," said Mr. Wilder-Smith. "I have important letters. Maybe you can help. But I must toddle along. Cheerio! Top-hole to meet you."

Mr. Wilder-Smith walked back along the wharf. Not a child spoke. They went right on fishing.

"Let's go!" said Henry. "Thanks, Eddie, for the fishing lessons."

"OK," said Eddie.

When the Aldens reached the sand, Jessie said, "Why do you suppose Freddy ever asked Mr. Carter to come with him?"

"Because he's a smart man," said Grandfather. "Freddy wants us to think he is honest. But he'll find that John Carter is smarter than he is."

Nobody on the wharf could hear what the Aldens said now. Benny said in a low voice, "Mr. Carter wanted to find some way to send us messages, didn't he—talking about the post office?"

"That's what I thought," said Jessie.

"I know a way," said Benny. "You know that old log on the beach that Grandfather sits on? There's a deep hole in one end. We can put a small piece of paper in the hole any time. And so can he."

"Good!" said Jessie. "Let's send him our message right away. The people know that we often sit on that log. They won't notice."

Henry wrote it. He made it as short as he could. "Light in schoolhouse at night. Back window has no lock. Broom closet goes into secret room in chimney. Look out of Washington's coat button."

"Now how shall we put it in the log?" asked Violet.

"I know!" said Jessie. "We'll make some sandwiches and have a picnic on the beach. While we are eating we can hide the paper."

The girls quickly made some cheese sandwiches. They packed the basket with many other things. Mr. Alden sat on the log. "Why don't you hide the paper yourself, Gramps?" said Benny. "You know where the hole is."

"Don't watch me," said Mr. Alden. Then in a minute he said, "It's all done." Not a sign of paper showed.

"I wonder how Mr. Carter will get it out?" said Benny.

"Well, that's his lookout," said Mr. Alden. "I wouldn't worry about him."

CHAPTER 12

A Sockful of Money

The picnic was over. The Aldens sat looking out over the blue water when the factory whistle blew.

"Oh, dear," said Benny. "Now everyone will go to work and nobody will be at home when Freddy comes."

"They don't all go to work," said Jessie. "By the way, I need some stuffing for the fish tonight. I'll go to the store while you take the picnic things home."

"I'll go for you, Jessie," said Benny. "I'd like to."

"Good boy," said Henry.

Benny walked up to the store, whistling. Mr. Fenton had the fish stuffing, and the two began to talk.

The door opened, and who should come in but Freddy Willet!

"Hello, kid," said Freddy. "I saw you come in. You one of the youngsters that teaches the funny school?"

"It isn't a funny school," said Benny with good nature. "And I do teach the smallest ones. They're pretty keen kids, too."

"Your name?" asked Mr. Willet.

"Benny."

"Well, Benny, how would you like to learn something yourself? Come with me to the Easton family and watch me buy their old money. I bet you don't know money when you see it. You'd never think a common penny was worth a dollar, would you?"

"No," said Benny. He kept wondering why Freddy had invited him and Mr. Wilder-Smith to watch while he cheated the people. Benny took his box of stuffing and the two walked over to the house where the Eastons lived.

Mrs. Easton was waiting at the door with a smile. At that moment Mr. Wilder-Smith came along.

"Well, here we all are," said Freddy. "Now you

can watch me work. Mrs. Easton, we are all happy to be here. Let's get started."

Benny could hardly believe his eyes when Mrs. Easton put an old stocking on the table and poured out a pile of money. Some of the coins were very old, and a few had hardly been used at all.

Mrs. Easton said, "Some of that money was saved by my grandfather."

They sat down at the table. Mr. Willet moved like lightning. He picked out one coin after another and dropped each in an empty box. He checked some coins by using a magnifying glass. Mr. Wilder-Smith just looked on. He did not seem to know a thing about coins.

"Is this an old penny?" asked Benny. It was almost as big as a half dollar, but it was made of copper.

"Yes, that's an old penny. Let's see. The date is 1864. I can pay Mrs. Easton ten dollars for it." He put a ten-dollar bill on the table and the penny in the box.

Mrs. Easton smiled and said, "Mr. Willet works fast. He knows his business."

"You can say that again!" said Freddy. He showed his teeth in a wide smile. He went on, "This is a nice job, Mr. Wilder-Smith. I have already bought five-hundred dollars worth of coins and things from these fishermen. They are very grateful to me."

"No wonder, old boy," said Mr. Wilder-Smith. "What in the world do you want them for?"

"Oh, I'm crazy about old things," said Freddy. "I like 'em all. But I like coins best."

Benny said, "I don't see how you remember the prices without a book."

"Easy!" said Freddy. "I've been at this business for many years. I know a coin the minute I see it."

"I say," said Mr. Wilder-Smith, "you might make a mistake."

"Not me," said Freddy. "I know these coins like old friends. I never make a mistake. There! This is the best one I've found."

He pushed a dime over to the two visitors. "Here is a new coin in perfect condition. But look at the date. 1901S. I'll pay Mrs. Easton plenty for that. She'll never forget Freddy Willet, you bet."

"I certainly won't," said Mrs. Easton.

"I'm sure of that," said Mr. Wilder-Smith. "That dime looks as if it had never been used."

"That's right. It never has been used. That dime has sat here for more than sixty years."

"By Jove, I thought a worn-out coin was worth more," said the Englishman.

"No, not if it's worn smooth. Then it's worth nothing. See this big copper penny? Smooth as silk. I can't read the date. That penny is old enough, but it's not worth a cent!" He laughed loudly at his own joke.

"That's all," said Freddy. "The rest are no good. I'll

just settle up with Mrs. Easton."

"Thanks very much," said Mr. Wilder-Smith. "It was a jolly good show. I learned a lot from you."

"I guess you learned something today, too, young man," said Freddy.

"Yes, I did," said Benny. He said goodbye to Mrs. Easton, and he and Mr. Wilder-Smith went out together.

Benny whispered quickly, "Hole in the log." And Mr. Wilder-Smith whispered, "Look three times a day."

Then Benny went one way and Mr. Wilder-Smith another. They did not seem to know each other, for the Englishman took off his hat to the boy.

Benny had a great deal to tell his family. He told it in a whisper.

Jessie said, "It's funny how we all whisper. It seems as if somebody is listening all the time."

"Maybe someone is," said Violet.

They were noisy enough when Jessie put the baked stuffed fish on the table. They had baked potatoes, too, and onions, and apple pie and cheese.

"A big dinner at last," said Benny. "I'm hungry."

When it grew dark, the Aldens sat out in the yard in front of the hotel. Henry was on one end. He turned suddenly as he heard a noise coming from the bushes behind the house. It was a whisper.

"Benny! Come with me to the schoolhouse. Bring the back door key. Follow me through the bushes." It was John Carter's voice.

They all heard it. Henry gave the key to his brother. Benny went without a sound.

"Why did he want Benny?" Jessie wondered.

"Maybe his small size is better than my big size," guessed Henry, speaking low. Then he began to talk about other things in his own tone of voice.

At ten o'clock Benny came back. He was very much excited.

"Whisper, Ben," said Henry. "Who knows who is listening?"

So Benny said in a whisper, "We tried the room in the chimney. We could both get in, and we could see right through the coat button into the schoolroom. Mr. Carter thinks Freddy is hiding things in the schoolroom. But we couldn't find them. He is going to hunt again. He thinks Freddy will stay a while longer because he has a lot of families left to visit."

"Well, well," said Mr. Alden. "You will have something to tell Max. It won't be dull, either."

"It's funny," said Benny. "We didn't do anything to make this happen."

"No, Benny," said his grandfather. "But you all kept your eyes open. You cared enough about your new friends to worry about them. And you listened when they told you about the man who paid so much for a quarter. You guessed that he was cheating in every trade."

"But we can't prove a thing," said Henry.

"No," said Grandfather. "That's why I am so glad to see John Carter."

CHAPTER 13

Surprise for Violet

The Aldens could hardly teach school on Monday with Mr. Willet making calls on every family in the village. All the children knew about it. They couldn't help talking about it. At recess they did not want to play. They wanted to talk.

"Oh, my ma's got an old gold pin with a lion's head on it," said one girl. "The Money Man's going to pay her real money for it. And she's got an old garnet ring, too."

"And my grandma's got a big box of old valentines," said her brother. "The Money Man is going to buy those."

"My pa has got an old tin dish they used to cut meat on," said Tommy Spoon.

"Could that be pewter?" asked Violet.

"Pewter? No, I never heard of that."

"And we've got an old hourglass they used in church over in Northport," said Eddie.

"We've got a glass paperweight full of flowers. The Money Man is just crazy over it," said another child.

Then suddenly Hal got up on a rock and began to talk. "You kids, listen here!" he began. "You got all the afternoon to talk about the Money Man. And this morning you got a good chance to learn something. We don't ever get any teachers like these Aldens, teaching us interesting things. And they won't be here much longer. Let's stop talking and learn. That's all I've got to say."

Some of the children clapped for Hal's speech, and soon everyone was busy. The morning flew by. Then Violet said, "Now let's paint. We can go down to the beach."

Marie and Hal were more excited than the other children. Marie begged, "Please teach me to paint the harbor the way the artist did."

"I'll help you as much as I can," Violet promised.

The girls and boys took their painting things down to the water. The Aldens helped them get started. Violet had Marie and Hal draw the harbor first with pencil. She showed them only one thing. She said, "Notice that the lines of the wharf look as if they get closer together as they stretch into the water."

As soon as Violet had shown the children how to hold their brushes she said, "Now paint away, just as you feel."

Soon Jessie and Henry came over by Violet to watch the Moss twins.

Both Hal and Marie dashed on blue and green paint that was just the right color for the sea. The boats that they made looked like real boats, but they were drawn with only a few lines. It was hard to believe that this was the first time the twins had had watercolors.

All at once Violet knew the truth. Here were two natural artists, much better than she would ever be. There was something different about their painting—something all their own.

Marie cried, "Oh, here's that purple place," and she splashed purple and black under the wharf. She was not careful at all. Her picture made Jessie exclaim, "Beautiful!"

Hal's picture was just as good, but it was different.

"May I take your paintings to show our grandfather?" Violet asked the twins.

"I could paint another!" cried Hal. "I know a different way to paint the ocean, the way it looks in a storm."

Just then Mr. Alden came walking along the beach to see what was going on. Violet ran to show Mr. Alden the two paintings.

"Well, well!" he said. "What have we here? Watercolors? These are really good! These artists ought to go to art school. Not now, but later."

School was over for the morning. The bell was ringing. Henry knew that Benny would soon lock the schoolroom door and come back to the beach.

"Old Ben wants his lunch," he said, laughing.

"So do I," said Mr. Alden. "I wish Benny would come."

As they were eating, Violet said slowly, "I think Miss Gray ought to see these paintings."

"Oh, so do I," said Benny. "I'm sure she'd like them."

After lunch the whole family set out with the two pictures. They climbed the cliff walk and rang Miss Gray's bell.

Eva opened the door. She laughed. "I don't have to ask any more when it's you," she said. "Come right in."

When Miss Gray saw the Aldens she really smiled. It was the first time the Aldens had seen her smile like this.

"How is Freddy?" she asked.

"Well, Freddy is getting into trouble," said Grandfather. "He is too brave. He is going a little too far."

"How about the books?"

Mr. Alden had to say, "We don't know yet about the books."

"I'm sure you will get them back," said Benny. "You see—"

Henry looked at his brother. Benny stopped.

Miss Gray said, "Yes? What were you going to say?"

"Well, I guess it wasn't important," said Benny. "We're watching Freddy most of the time." Benny was not sure what Miss Gray knew about her English guest.

Mr. Alden said, "We really came to show you two watercolors. We'd like to know what you think of them." He passed them to Miss Gray.

"The harbor," said Miss Gray. "Very good. Were they done by one artist or two?"

"Two," said Violet with bright eyes. "The twins, Hal and Marie Moss."

"Hal and Marie!" said Miss Gray. "They never had a lesson!"

"No," said Grandfather, "they were born that way."

Jessie said, "They have seen only three paintings in their lives. An artist came here long ago and painted their house and the harbor. And there's George Washington in the schoolroom."

"That's why they have a style of their own," said

Miss Gray with a nod.

Violet said, "We have to go home the first of August. Somebody ought to look after those twins."

Miss Gray looked straight at Violet. "I will," she said. Then she seemed to be having a hard time with her words. At last she said, "When you go home, I'm going to teach your school myself."

"You?" cried Jessie. "Are you strong enough?"

"I'm strong enough," said Miss Gray. "Those twins live in my own town, and here I sit writing books. Nobody ever knew those children could paint. If you hadn't come along, I don't believe anyone would ever have found them."

The Aldens started to go. Miss Gray went to the door with them. As Grandfather bowed to her, she said, "Mr. Alden, Violet found the two artists, and your Benny found *me*."

CHAPTER 14

Caught!

The next day everyone saw Freddy Willet coming and going about the island in his red sports car. But no one ever saw him open the trunk, and there were no boxes in the front of the car.

"He must be hiding the library books in the schoolhouse," said Benny. "There's no other place here where he could hide the bigger things he has traded. But Mr. Carter can't find a thing."

Henry looked serious. "Time is getting short," he said. "In another day or two Freddy will have everything of value that can be found on this island."

After supper the Aldens found a long note hidden in the hollow log on the beach. In it John Carter said,

"Fred Willet is Harold K. Frederic. He has two other names he also uses. Canadian police want him for smuggling. All we have to do is get him to the border."

That evening the Aldens sat outside their hotel as they always did. When it was quite dark, they grew more and more excited. They were sure something was going to happen. They were not at all surprised to hear a whisper: "Benny, follow me."

While the others talked about the weather, Benny slipped after John Carter.

At first Benny thought that the schoolhouse was dark. Then he saw that something had been hung over a window. It was a car blanket. A dim light showed through another window.

Without a word, John Carter and Benny crept in at the back door. They went into the tiny chimney room. Mr. Carter looked through the hole in Washington's coat button. He let Benny look.

The room was faintly lighted by a square flashlight on one of the desks in the back of the room. At first Benny could not tell what Freddy Willet was doing.

Then he saw. The man was taking the wood out of the woodbox!

"His hiding place!" whispered Mr. Carter. "Now let me look."

When all the wood was out of the woodbox, Mr. Willet turned the box upside down very carefully and poured coin after coin on the back desk. He swept them quickly into a strong bag.

"The books?" whispered Benny.

Mr. Carter shook his head. Then he was really surprised. Mr. Willet went to the bookcase that held

the school books and took them all out. He took out a board in the back of the bookcase. Then he began to take out the old books from the library.

Mr. Carter stepped aside to let Benny look through the hole. Book after book came out of the space behind the shelf. Then came the doll, the buttons, the gold pins, the iron bank—everything.

Benny was thinking hard. "Mr. Willet must have been in the schoolhouse many times before. It took a long time to fix that hole behind the school books. That's what he was doing when we couldn't find him. My, what a lot of books! What will he do with them?"

He soon found out. Freddy took six books and began to tie them up with string. He set them on another desk. Soon he had sixty books. Then he put the board back, and fixed the school books just as they had been.

Mr. Carter took Benny's place at the peephole. He was not a minute too soon, for Freddy took some books in one hand and was reaching to put out the flashlight when he heard Mr. Carter's voice.

"Hold it, Willet! Don't move! The front door is locked now!"

Mr. Carter and Benny dashed down the back hall and into the schoolroom. Mr. Willet did the only thing he could do. He put out his light.

But this did him no good, for when his light went out, Mr. Carter's went on.

"What's the matter with you?" shouted Freddy. "I haven't done anything!"

"Oh, yes, you have!" said John Carter. "Just put those books down. What about all the little things you traded? What about the coins?"

"They were fair trades!" shouted Freddy. "Everyone was satisfied. They were glad to trade."

"That's because they did not know the things were antiques," said Mr. Carter. "And what about these books? A trade?"

"I borrowed those books. You just sign your name and take what you want. And I signed mine!"

"Which name did you sign, Freddy?" asked Mr. Carter softly.

Then Freddy knew he was in trouble. He had three

or four names, and John Carter knew every one of them. Mr. Carter went on. "The Canadian police want you, Freddy. They will be very glad to see you. You have been smuggling for years. You made a great mistake to try it again. No, leave all the things right where they are!"

Mr. Willet made one last try. "You aren't a policeman. You can't arrest me." He was very angry.

"You're wrong," said John Carter. "I was made a special policeman a week ago in Northport. But you'll be glad to know that the chief of police from Northport is sitting in your red car out in the bushes."

That stopped Freddy for a minute. Then he said, "Now, listen! I've paid these people a lot of money for old coins."

"Not enough," said John Carter. "You were going to sell the coins to the Adams College Museum. We can do that for you, and thanks very much for picking out the best ones!"

"You'll have to pay me back what I paid," said Freddy.

"We will, in time," said Mr. Carter. "Nobody is

going to cheat you, Freddy. But money won't do you much good in prison. Ah, hello, Anderson! Benny and I are glad to see you."

A tall policeman from Northport had come in the back door.

Freddy growled, "The Alden kids did this!"

"Yes," agreed Mr. Carter, "the Alden kids did this. They did their duty as American citizens. They just did what was right."

Mr. Anderson said to Benny, "We all thank you, and so will Canada. We have tried for years to catch Mr. North."

"Mr. North!"

"Yes, and Mr. Frederic and Mr. Benson. They are all Freddy Willet. We will go in his own car."

Freddy Willet was smart. He knew when he was caught. He went with the policeman without another word. It was low tide, just as Freddy had planned, and the road to Canada was straight before the two men.

Standing outside the hotel, Grandfather, Henry, Jessie, and Violet saw the car disappear over the stones and gravel to the mainland.

CHAPTER 15

The Last Song

What excitement there was in Port Elizabeth when the people heard about Freddy! It was hard for them to believe that the Money Man had cheated them. But when Mr. Carter told them that just one of the old valentines was worth many dollars, they changed their minds.

"Oh, it seems wonderful to talk out loud again," said Benny. "I don't like to have people hiding and listening and whispering. Now I can yell if I want to."

"It's good to talk to you again, Mr. Carter," said Henry, "and no Mr. Wilder-Smith."

"What did you find out at Adams College, John?" asked Grandfather.

"They want to buy many of the coins," said Mr. Carter. "And I found two collectors who want the rest. I am going to call on every family and pay them the right price for their coins."

"What a job!" said Henry.

"All in a day's work," Mr. Carter said with a smile.

"What about the little things?" asked Jessie.

"I will give them all back," said Mr. Carter. "An honest antique dealer will come up here a little later. The people can sell them or keep them, whatever they wish."

"Mr. Willet did give Marie a red necklace," said Benny slowly.

Mr. Carter smiled. "That necklace cost him twenty-five cents," he said. "I guess you don't need to worry about that."

Violet said suddenly, "Maybe Miss Gray would like to sell her old books to an honest man. Nobody here reads them."

"Right, Violet," said Mr. Carter. "That's exactly what she told me. But she said a lot more. She thought she was foolish to think anybody would read them. She plans to buy a whole library of colored picture books, stories, and other new books. The books will be for both children and grown-ups."

"Good," said Jessie. "She has changed, and now she's really wonderful."

The Aldens had planned to have a picnic for the school children on the last day. But no—the children wanted to go to school!

"What children!" said Violet. "I never saw any children like them anywhere."

As the children were singing a last song, someone came in the back door. The children could hardly believe their eyes. They clapped without knowing it. They had seen Miss Gray only from a distance, but they knew who she was.

Henry said, "Miss Gray is going to be your teacher until a new one comes. And she will choose somebody to ring the bell."

"We won't say goodbye," said Benny. "We hate to

say goodbye. We never do, we just go."

It was hard, but everyone did just go. Mr. Alden sat outside in the station wagon. Miss Gray's gardener took her home. The Aldens piled into the station wagon, and the school children waved and waved. Then the car rattled over the rocks and stones, and the Aldens were soon on their way home.

When they reached home, Benny called up his friend Max.

"Hello, Max! It's me!"

"Oh, hi, Ben! How about adventures? Did you catch a thief or find hidden treasure?"

"Both!" said Benny. "Come over on your bike and we'll tell you all about the thief and the money hidden in old socks."

"Don't try to fool me, Ben," said Max. "You couldn't find all that on such a dull island."

"Well, we did," said Benny. "It was so exciting that we could hardly pay attention to our schoolteaching."

"Schoolteaching! Are you crazy?"

"No," said Benny. "We did more than that. We

met a famous author and we discovered two artists."

"I don't believe it," said Max. But he always believed Benny Alden.

It was not long before Max leaned his bike against the front steps. The Aldens took turns telling him about the schoolhouse mystery.

"It's too much," said Max at last. "I've been up there two summers. And not a thing happened except that we ate our meals and went fishing. Not a thing! But, Mr. Alden, I thought you were going to take the family somewhere else this summer?"

"Well, so I am, Max," said Grandfather. He winked.

"Not much time left, sir."

"There's enough. There's all of August and part of September," said Mr. Alden.

"Almost time to go to the moon," said Benny.